This book is for

_____

With love from

_____

On this date

_____

ZONDERKIDZ

Every Breath, Every Blessing

Copyright © 2025 Dorena Williamson
Illustrations © 2025 Dorena Williamson

Published by Zonderkidz, 3950 Sparks Drive, Suite 101, Grand Rapids, Michigan, 49546. Zonderkidz is a registered trademark of The Zondervan Corporation, L.L.C., a wholly owned subsidiary of HarperCollins Christian Publishing, Inc.

Requests for information should be addressed to customercare@harpercollins.com.

ISBN 978-0-310-16678-8 (hardcover)
ISBN 978-0-310-16679-5 (ebook)
ISBN 978-0-310-17848-4 (audio)

Library of Congress Cataloging-in-Publication Data

Names: Williamson, Dorena, author. | Kim, Paran, illustrator.
Title: Every breath, every blessing / by Dorena Williamson ; illustrated by Paran Kim.
Description: Grand Rapids : Zonderkidz, [2025]. | Audience: Ages 4 and up. | Summary: "A gentle story of affirmation and love, Every Breath, Every Blessing is a message of reassurance for the big feelings and questions that children face in uncertain times, reminding them to cherish the life they have been given"-- Provided by publisher.
Identifiers: LCCN 2024021636 (print) | LCCN 2024021637 (ebook) | ISBN 9780310166788 (hardcover) | ISBN 9780310166795 (ebook)
Subjects: LCSH: Affirmations--Juvenile fiction. | Parent and child--Juvenile fiction. | Emotions in children--Juvenile fiction. | Conduct of life--Juvenile fiction. | CYAC: Parent and child--Fiction. | Emotions--Fiction. | Conduct of life--Fiction. | LCGFT: Picture books.
Classification: LCC PZ7.1.W5553 Ev 2025 (print) | LCC PZ7.1.W5553 (ebook) | DDC 813.6 [E]--dc23/eng/20241121
LC record available at https://lccn.loc.gov/2024021636
LC ebook record available at https://lccn.loc.gov/2024021637

No part of this publication may be reproduced, stored in a retrieval system, or transmitted in any form or by any means—electronic, mechanical, photocopy, recording, or any other—except for brief quotations in printed reviews, without the prior permission of the publisher.

Published in association with the literary agency of WTA Media, LLC., Franklin, Tennessee.

Zondervan titles may be purchased in bulk for educational, business, fundraising, or sales promotional use. For information, please email SpecialMarkets@Zondervan.com.

Edited by: Katherine Jacobs and Jacque Alberta
Art direction: Patti Evans
Interior design: Kristen Sasamoto
Illustrated by: Paran Kim

Printed in Batu Tiga, Malaysia

25 26 27 28 29 / OFF / 5 4 3 2 1

Every Breath, Every Blessing

FINDING HOPE ON TOUGH DAYS

Written by
DORENA WILLIAMSON

Illustrated by
PARAN KIM

My precious child,
let's take a moment together.

Breathe in—
    you are alive.
Breathe out—
    you are so loved.

Of the millions and billions of people across the world,
you are a one-of-a-kind design created in love by the Giver of Breath.

Life is one of His precious blessings,
and while we are living,
happiness can flow like a peaceful river
or sadness can come in on rolling waves.

In those hard times,
I wish we could snap our fingers
and find ourselves in a faraway land
full of only goodness and peace.

But right here, right now, know this:
When storms shake everything up,
we can wait them out together,
and I will pray for you whenever we are apart.

Breathe in—
    your life is a blessing.
Breathe out—
    you are more valuable than
    the creatures in the sky.

We can always talk about anything
or just sit together in silence.
I promise to be honest with you
even when I don't know the answers to
your questions.

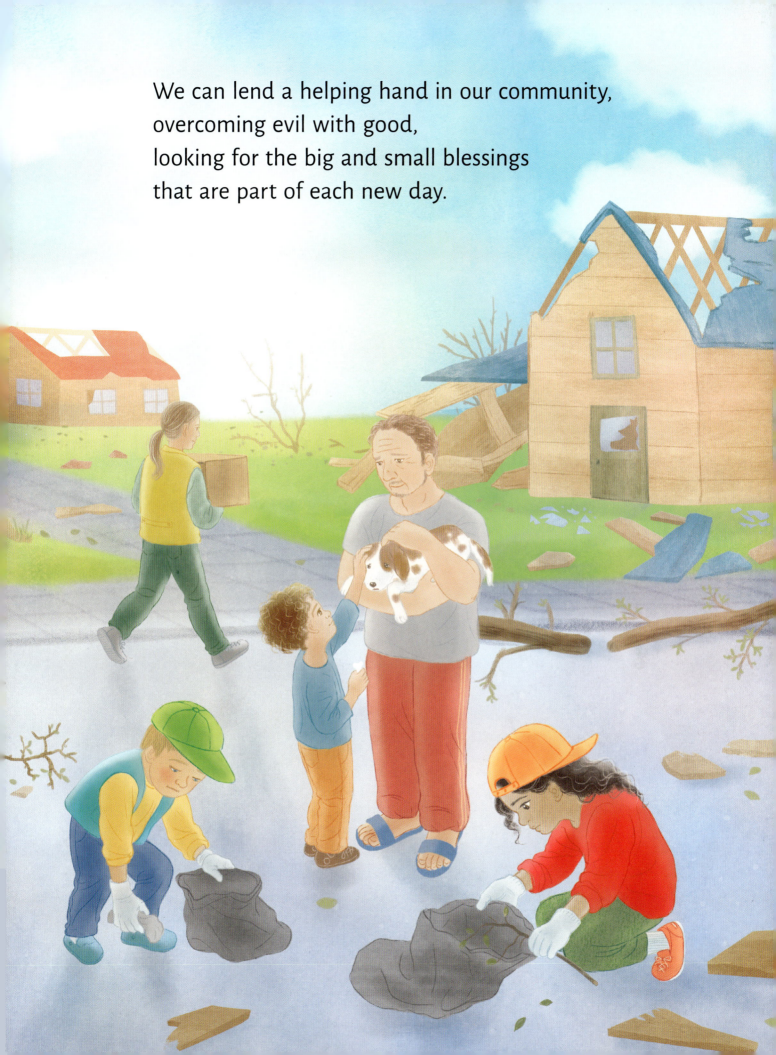

We can lend a helping hand in our community,
overcoming evil with good,
looking for the big and small blessings
that are part of each new day.

Sometimes your feelings of fear, joy, doubt, excitement tumble around like a bouncy ball, giving you energy. Other times those same feelings might sit like a rock in your stomach, giving you anxiety.

If there is trouble,
follow the directions and drills you have learned.
If I am not with you, look for the helpers.
They care about your safety too.

You can't always control what others may do,
but YOU can do this:
Breathe in—
    you can control yourself.
Breathe out—
    do the next right thing.

Together,
we are going to take life one day at a time.

For every breath,
count every blessing.
Breathe in.
    My life is worth living.

Breathe out.
I will make every day count.